The Larvae, Ansaldo and The Spice Merchant's Son

Robert Zola Christensen

Translated by Nina Sokol

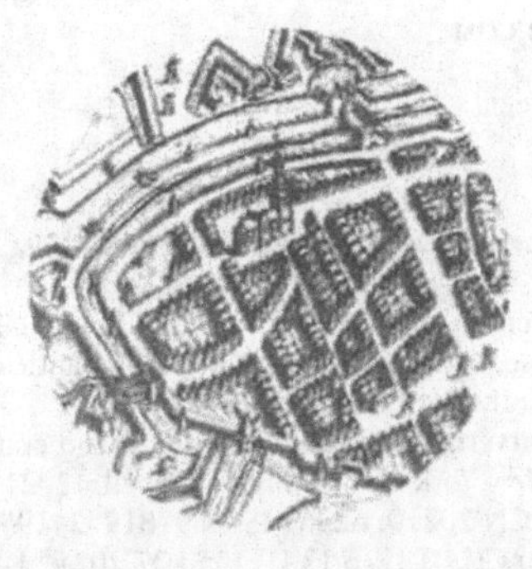

SPUYTEN DUYVIL

New York City

Special thanks to The Danish Arts Foundation for financial
support towards the translation and publication of this book.

Danish Arts
Foundation

Library of Congress Cataloging-in-Publication Data

Names: Christensen, Robert Zola, author. | Sokol, Nina, translator.
Title: The larvae, Ansaldo and the spice merchant's son / Robert Zola
  Christensen ; translated by Nina Sokol.
Other titles: Larverne, Ansaldo og krydderihandlerens søn. English
Description: New York City : Spuyten Duyvil, [2021] |
Identifiers: LCCN 2021006296 | ISBN 9781952419591 (paperback)
Classification: LCC PT8176.13.H7355 L37 2021 | DDC 839.813/74--dc23
LC record available at https://lccn.loc.gov/2021006296

THE LARVAE,

ANSALDO

AND THE SPICE MERCHANT'S SON

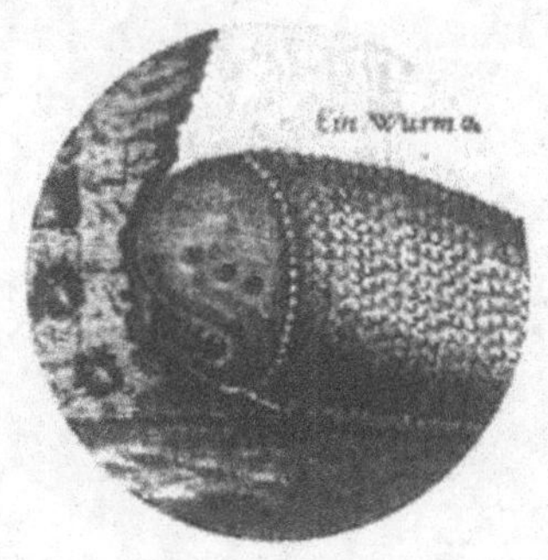

0:A

I
THE PLAGUE

JUST LIKE IN PARIS, there are men in Calais who deal in human trafficking. They frequent the bars at the harbor to see if there are any newcomers. I was sitting together with my two travel companions, the spice merchant's son and the man from Rouen. We were in the middle of eating a meal which consisted of meat and cabbage when an elderly sailor entered. He sat down at the end of the table and started interrogating us. He wanted to know where we came from and how tall we were.

Then he ordered some Spanish wine and said that if we for a brief moment took the trouble of looking down at the harbor we would see that at this very instant there was what he described a gorgeous ship a little offshore. It was to disembark for Martinique in seven or eight days, he continued, and wouldn't it be something to come and see the passengers aboard?

Where are you headed, Frenchie? he asked me before we had a chance to respond.

When I told him that most of the women in my hometown village had been afflicted by the plague and that I was on my way out into the world to find a bride, he said it was just a matter of getting on that boat to Martinique, Fort-de-France, where the women were truly exceptional.

As tempting as that sounded, it wouldn't do, was my response, I am making my way up North where a distant branch of the family has found a suitable woman for me.

What about you, philosopher? he then asked the man

from Rouen who, for whatever reason, had introduced himself as a philosopher.

I intervened and made a correction. I made it clear that the man from Rouen was a private tutor and that the only reason why he was traveling with me was because he was going to teach my bride-to-be to speak the impossibly difficult French language that was my mother-tongue.

Well, you could at least accompany me down to the ship and try to walk on its wide planks, the sailor said as he looked round the table. And then he mentioned what he himself referred to as the mother of all baits: the big canons.

Before we knew it we had gone down with him to the harbor where a small boat was waiting to row us out to the ship. Two big strapping men sat ready at the oars. The first of us to jump on board was the spice merchant's son followed by the man from Rouen. When it was my turn, I suddenly stopped in my tracks, keeping my one foot on land. I had a clear sense that things weren't quite as they seemed.

Come on! One of the oarsmen said, we don't have all day. The man from Rouen, who was sitting in the boat next to the elderly sailor looked up at me. Then he crawled back onto land and positioned himself next to me.

The elderly sailor pointed toward the ship that lay in the sunlight and tried to tempt us by telling us about all the good food and Rostock-beer waiting for us if we joined them. I told him that I had made up my mind.

The spice merchant's son sat all the way up front in the boat smiling his strange smile that had haunted me ever since we had left our hometown village. I motioned to him to get out of the boat and come up to us, but he didn't. And then they started rowing. The man from Rouen and I watched them as they headed out to sea. The spice merchant's son waved at us several times and straightened his sweater, looking as if there was something wrong with us.

We returned to the pub and ordered more Spanish wine for the money that the man from Rouen said he had received for his horse earlier that week. The owner's wife, who had watched us leave, said that she was surprised to see that we had returned at all. She said that had we gone on-board the ship there was no telling what would have happened to us. We would most likely have been taken down into the hold of the ship, she said, and once we had been down there and seen the canons we would have discovered that the ship had started to sail away with us. We looked down at the harbor and to our horror we saw that that was exactly what was taking place at that very moment. They had started to set sail and were already on their way, leaving land behind.

I can still recall the spice merchant's son sitting there in the boat, waving and waving at us, and, to be honest, at that point I didn't think I was ever going to see him again, but, as fate would have it, I would.

I:A

WHAT IS THAT? I asked my future father-in-law who, while sipping a brown elixir, was squinting his eyes so tightly that it made his eyebrows knit together in a frown. It wasn't a pretty sight.

It's a grog, was his response, which I bought from an individual, Zobowski, from Lithuania. Even though the price of it per month corresponds to 400 kilos copper, I must drink two of these per day to keep my inner fluids in balance. When the liquid spreads through my organism I become as meek as a lamb and manage to forget all the ugliness of the world.

I presumed that I knew where the root of his worries derived from. His wife, who was more beautiful than their daughter, would carry a big pitcher with ointment each day to the camp hospital to treat a wounded soldier and when she returned she always carried the smell of another man on her which could be detected a mile away. As everyone knows, no man can bear being cuckolded.

It turned out, however, that its cause was rooted in something entirely different.

The mine owner's nostrils quivered as he told me that there had been an accident in the mine that had been of such magnitude that it had managed to distort physical reality as we know and feel it out of proportion.

How so? I wanted to know. I didn't understand what he meant.

Yes, well, you see, he explained, approximately a week

ago several pick axes and spades managed to break through the surface of an old well whereupon large amounts of water flooded into the mine which ran further down into the shaft. And when the water was gone there lay a large white larva worming its way through the heavy mud.

I remember this conversation taking place in the kitchen, one of the biggest rooms in the house. Through the window I could see my bride-to-be outside together with the man from Rouen, they were hacking a hole in the frozen lake. They wanted to fish. That is to say, the philosopher wanted to fish. Even though he should really have been fulfilling his duties as a private tutor he much preferred to poke for fish. He had also insisted that I use the moniker philosopher when referring to him, to which I had agreed.

When I again turned my attention to my future father-in-law it was to hear his response as to what the larva looked like and whether there was any possible chance that I could see it. I still hadn't understood the full story.

He answered that it resembled one of those eels that are usually thrown down in wells to consume insects and keep the water clean and which, if it is left to swim in the black water for a considerable amount of time, ends up becoming luminous and transparent and getting big protruding eyes. He also said that it was being preserved in a bucket down at the mine so it was fully possible for me to see it if that was what I wished. It is, was my answer.

In which case I would like to emphasize, he said as he emptied the last drops from the clay bottle, that it is in no way the animal's appearance that is of interest but rather that which it contains and the effect it has on its surroundings.

Outside the window I could see that the philosopher had

finally managed to hack through the ice and that he had hardly lowered the line before there was a bite on the other end. I now watched as the philosopher pulled something or other up from the water that was black and that hung completely still from the line without wriggling and I saw, without being able to see, what it was and that he began studying it. Then he looked down into the dark hole from which the catch had come. And then he looked with bewilderment up at the sky.

Later that day I began to realize that the world I thought I had known had truly cracked and broken into pieces: first cracked and then broken into pieces.

I:B

A BIRD. They had caught a bird and brought it inside. I could see it lying there on the bare stone floor in front of the hearth. At first it could only move its one wing but gradually it came more and more to life and after being in the warm indoors it managed to thaw out completely and started walking around in the kitchen. But it was still very unstable on its scrawny legs.

Of course I wanted an explanation as to what I was observing and, not so surprisingly, it was the philosopher who felt an obligation to provide me with one.

Whenever you see an effect there is always a cause and everything is connected, he began. The bird is a swallow which you can determine by looking at its wings which are long and slender. It is fit for a life in the air and not in the water which means it must belong to a flock that got off to a slightly late start on their way to a warmer climate and may have grown tired due to the cold weather. So they took a short rest on the shores of your lake. They landed on the tall rushes and when too many birds settled down on the same straw, well, it started to bend and the birds were practically poured down into the lake where they landed at the very bottom. And so now they're down there where they can survive without eating until someone fishes them up or spring comes. I've also read about flies that form clusters in the walls of houses or in thick moss on trees. They are actually able to get though the winter that way.

The mine owner first looked at me and then at the

philosopher before saying the following: Join me on the hunt tomorrow and I'll show you something you won't easily forget.

We had completely forgotten the swallow during our conversation. It had started to fly around in the high-ceilinged room, flapping its wings uncontrollably. First it hit the wall, then the lamp, crapping yellow excrement from sheer fear. At one point it flew out of an open window somewhere at the very top. Naturally we ran out to look for it. It made it above the lake and above the tall, slender trees the Swedes would use to make ship's masts and for a moment I actually thought it was going to make it but the poor, warmed-blooded animal wasn't made for the cold winter climate so suddenly it fell to the ground like a stone that had been tossed in the air.

THERE IT IS, the mine owner said to us, pointing in the direction of the trees to the place where he believed the armadillo he was so eager to show us was crawling around. But I couldn't see it. I simply couldn't catch sight of it. And apparently the philosopher couldn't either, but that didn't seem to bother the mine owner.

I saw it for myself a few weeks ago, he continued. My rifle was loaded and filled with duck-shot and under normal circumstances it would have been no problem catching up with it and shooting it. But it was. It was a big and inexplicable problem. Had it not been for the fact that I had seen it with my own eyes I would never have believed it.

I remember looking for it in vain among the trees as the mine owner continued speaking.

I released my pointer, he said, and let it chase the animal in the course of what became hours before whistling for it to return. It has been known to overtake every animal of the forest and when I say every I mean every. But not this time. It was hardly able to drag itself home afterward. Had I not lifted it up onto the back of my horse it would most probably have died from sheer exhaustion.

Take a good look now, the mine owner replied, pointing once again, and this time I did actually catch sight of something that moved and that something was a small armadillo stirring in the leaves. Then it suddenly started walking a little sideways up the tree trunk only to fall on its back and continued to do so.

I asked what in the world it was that we were witnessing. The philosopher, who normally wasn't at a loss for words, was rendered speechless.

Like all other armadillos, the mine owner responded, this one has two rows of legs below its belly, however, unlike others, this one has two rows on its back as well. When the row of legs below its belly grow tired it simply turns on its back and continues running with its row of numerous, well-rested legs.

THAT EVENING in his chamber, the philosopher took out the three reference books which he never traveled without and in *Grösste Denkwürdigkeiten der Welt oder Sogenannte Relationes Curiosæ*, which was chock-full of information and ornamental copper engravings, he found a description of a type of larva, Lapis Larvae, which, according to the reference, tended to live in mines and which, according to the philosopher, could easily be in the same family as the armadillo we had just seen.

We discussed the subjects of zoology and biology in great depth for quite a while and just as I had bidden him goodnight and was ready to retire, the philosopher said, There is nothing in our consciousness that hasn't first been processed through our senses. What do you mean? I asked. We humans can transform the surroundings in which we live, he began. We can cultivate corn on a bare field and we can fell trees and build houses. We are therefore inclined to believe that we are equipped with a consciousness that makes us capable of such actions on the basis of certain significant considerations when, in fact, the reality of the situation is the exact opposite. How is it opposite? I asked. The fact of the matter is is that it is due to our interference with and transformation of our reality that human consciousness grows. It emerges, to a certain degree, out of nothing.

The way in which the philosopher presented his statement struck me as something other and more than just a whim on his part and it made me hold back. I understood that it was a response to something the mine owner had said earlier. For during the dinner he had expressed the opinion that certain phenomena occurred which couldn't be justified on explanations solely based on reason and human awareness and which are beyond the known forces of nature.

Now that those events are so far behind me I can add that it was this disagreement which became the basis for the conflict between the two men that would later culminate in a wild bet and I cannot help thinking that it was a trap set up for him and which the philosopher walked straight into with his square toed shoes.

For his part, the philosopher insisted that it was solely a figment of the mine owner's imagination and that his notion of being attacked by some evil force or other was precisely what the evil force consisted of, in other words, he was suffering from a kind of spiritual disease that automatically fed on itself.

For my own part there is no denying that I was oddly attracted to those things that were unfamiliar to me and even though I could neither back then nor now claim that I entirely understood the essence of the philosopher's postulations, I took the liberty of saying that I, in spite of everything, wished to see the larva in question with my own eyes.

The most striking thing about Lapis Larvae is that which it consumes, the philosopher said. And what exactly would that be? I asked. It is the only known animal in the world to live off of consuming rocks.

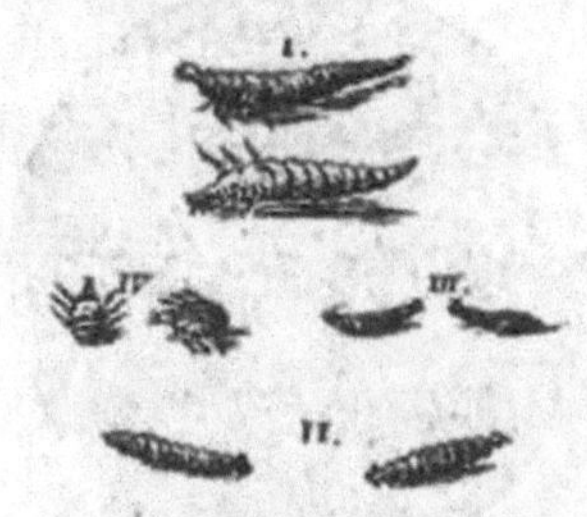

I:C

II
THE MINE

II:A

WE WERE STANDING NEXT TO a big tub that was filled with liquid copper and we were given sugared schnapps based on grain to help keep warm. It was so unbelievably cold, so different from Denmark where I have been now for almost a week.

Over by the hole the biggest of the workers was busy preparing the crane for us. He was dressed in black leather from head to foot and even his face was covered by a semi-mask of sorts that reached way down his chest.

Some black smoke rose from below the ground that had the faint smell of sulfur. I remember thinking that it resembled the opening to hell. I also remember thinking that we had made the right decision. We had to kill that larva-looking creature if it was at the root of the current situation. The philosopher didn't agree. During breakfast he had said outright that he couldn't stand listening to such peasant mumbo-jumbo and he therefore chose to stay home. I'd rather stick my fingers in my ears, were the exact words he used.

The black shaft-overseer waved us over and we crawled up in the braided basket. The two brown, fuming oxen that were to pull the hoisting device began to move.

Cold and dirty raindrops started coming down as we were slowly lowered down into the darkness. I assume it was snow that was melting. The ride took over half an hour with the basket hitting the sides every now and then. Orders were shouted both from above and below.

In the underground space we arrived in the walls were smooth and wet.

I crawled out of our means of transportation and looked around. The men I saw were bare-chested and wore leather pants and they were pushing wagon loads of iron ore, equipment and food in various directions.

The mine owner informed me that most of them were prison workers as well as sinners that due to crimes they had committed in previous lives would first be able to emerge to the daylight of real life when they had served their time. He added that it was seldom that they actually managed to survive for that long. Which didn't surprise me. And by the look of most of the men you could tell that they didn't really believe it either.

I followed the mine owner into the tunnel that tilted sharply downward. At first it was very wide but it gradually grew increasingly narrow and cramped. All across the mine ceiling there were lanterns that hung from wooden beams and supports. Everything was dripping with moisture.

After about 50 meters the mine tunnel seemed to reach a dead end where a small man stood working on his own. He was busy fixing the pothole that had emerged in the wall when the well broke. While the mine owner spoke with him I took the opportunity to thoroughly look him over. His head was wrapped in dirty, white bandages, so that practically all that was visible were his two two big round eyes protruding from his small face. There was a narrow slit in the middle of his face through which food could pass.

I assumed that he had gotten his injuries in connection with the accident. I never received an answer regarding that, but it was, of course, nothing compared to what he would have to endure later.

When the mine owner placed his hand on the man's shoulder with a chumminess which I found somewhat inappropriate I asked him where the larva was located. The whole reason why we had come there was to cut off its head. I had at that point already noted that the wooden bucket standing on the floor was empty.

Instead of answering my question my father-in-law-to-be began telling how he had managed to purchase the freedom of Ansaldo in an Italian town two years earlier.

I was in the small town square, he said, where I was busy smelling at the cheeses when Ansaldo and another criminal were escorted to the scaffold amidst the cries of a cheering crowd. I immediately noticed that Ansaldo possessed precisely those qualities that a job of this kind requires. I am the kind of man who, when he sees a hook hanging from the ceiling can't help wondering what it could be used for, so I decided to take him with me back to Sweden along with all my new cheeses.

I repeated my question: Where is the larva?

Ansaldo looked at me with his protruding eyes whereupon he replied in excellent French, which was nonetheless influenced by Italian, that it had escaped from the bucket and had probably joined the other members of its species who had been flushed further down in the mine along with the water that had entered it. Now I was seriously confused. I thought there was only one larva we had to kill. Now suddenly there were several. And what was even worse: we didn't know where they were.

I expressed my concern which prompted the Italian to show me that at the place in which the mine tunnel ended there was an opening, or rather, a free-fall that led further down to the underground. I carefully leaned forward but couldn't see anything even though I strained my eyes to the utmost degree. They are swimming around down there, Ansaldo said. All the fish larvae. And there were more than I had time to count when they floated past here about a week ago.

I asked how deep it was, but he didn't know. I took a stone and threw it down into the darkness and what seemed like an eternity passed before it finally made a splash as it hit the water. I could see that the sides of the hole were equipped with tiny steps of wood, so I considered crawling down there.

But before I decided whether or not to go down I heard a bell. It had a loud tone and sounded like it came from everywhere. It was being transmitted throughout the mine tunnels. I didn't know what it was and I feared that it might be in connection with a collapse or a gas slippage. I started running back toward the place where we had crawled from the basket. Ansaldo and the mine owner remained standing as they watched me depart.

IT TURNED OUT THAT THE little bell I had heard while we had been in the underground wasn't an alarm, as I had initially feared, but a signal indicating that something or other of the greatest interest had been discovered in the mine. Which was precisely what it was. It wasn't the usual find which normally consisted of copper, but a beautiful marble coffin. It was shaped like an angel. It almost took an hour to maneuver it up from the hole in the ground and an additional three to drag it home to the mine owner. My guess is that it weighed more than the three horses that pulled it through the snow on the big sleigh. Looking back on it today I think it is safe to say that we were just as idiotic as the Trojans were when they dragged the wooden figure which Odysseus had filled with Greek soldiers into their fortress

The coffin was placed in the living room and turned chalk-white once it was properly rinsed off. Next, some handymen from the nearest village attempted to remove the lid. They used every tool they had but it was no use. Then the philosopher took over. He thoroughly examined the sarcophagus. He crawled around on it, listened to it, and he tapped on it with a small wooden hammer. Afterward he summoned the whole household in the living room. I recall how we were seated on hard furniture along the wall. The philosopher stood in the middle of the room with the coffin before him. Somewhat unnecessarily, he began by saying that the dark corners of the human mind ought to be illuminated through studying and the practice of independent thinking. Whereupon he delivered the message to us that he had reached the conclusion that there was, in fact, something inside there, that it wasn't just empty. He also said that it presumably hadn't been opened for many centuries.

Then I took the floor. I even rose to my feet. I said that that couldn't come as a surprise. Why create such a beautiful object without filling it up with something since that was what it was designed for? Whereupon I sat back down.

The philosopher, who has a long and lanky physiognomy, drummed his fingers on his chin as he circled the coffin.

The thing is, he said, is that I am convinced that whatever is inside of it is moving. It is alive.

Naturally we discussed a great deal what it could possibly be. On the other hand, we didn't talk so much about what we actually planned to do with the larvae which, in retrospect, I must confess was a big mistake. The discovery of the coffin was to prove to be an unwelcome distraction that would yield disastrous consequences and I cannot deny putting a good part of the blame on the philosopher.

It must be added, however, that preparations for my own wedding were at that point well under way and contributed greatly to the fact that everything else tended to fade into the background. The wedding was to take place a week later and I knew that all the members of the family, who hailed from many different places, had already commenced their journey to Falun. The servants had already begun to heat up the extra houses and dwelling places that belonged to the estate. I might also mention that side wings and other forms of construction had rather unsystematically popped up out of the ground at the same time that the mine owner was busy fetching copper and iron ore from the underground. There had even been put up a bathing hut, a mill and a chapel. The one thing that made it all connect was the high wall which he had had built around his entire property. A week later in the process that wall would prove to be the one thing that saved us.

I still haven't written anything more about my bride-to-be, but there is a good reason for that. Everything that came out of her mouth was heavy-sounding in my ears and when I said flattering things to her it was for no other reason than to say them. I will be the first to admit that she had a pretty enough face, however, she also happened to be five centimeters taller than me and had heavy thighs and calves. There was also something about her behavior which I found to be unsuitable for a wife. She resembled her mother.

When I entered the library one afternoon where the philosopher was busy teaching about Euclid's doctrine and Pascal she rose to her feet and curtseyed clumsily to me. When she then sat back down on the bench she did it in such a way that her dress crept up and revealed the hair on her genitalia. Although it is natural for the tame mare to let its tail swing to the side when the stallion is led into the stable, I did not in the least bit care for what I had seen.

II:B

We played Cadrille during the dark afternoons and evenings which there were two reasons for. It turned out that my fiance and her mother enjoyed passing the time playing card games at the same time that the climate there allowed us only to a very limited degree to play nine pins or engage in other outdoor activities which both the philosopher and I would have appreciated.

One evening as we were were sitting around the card table there arose a dispute between the mine owner, who had a stubborn nature, and the man from Rouen. The discussion had to do with the recent events that had occurred in Falun. The philosopher refused to hear any talk of the incident being a supernatural phenomenon.

Nature is a great and beautiful machine, he said. There is always a new and sensible explanation for everything and even though it may be difficult to find you can be sure that it will be convincing once you do. Everything else is merely heresy. When the head sticks out we place a hat on it and since legs are equipped, as they are, with flat feet it is because you are supposed to walk on them.

Whereupon the philosopher pointed at my fiance's hand which was holding the cards with spread fingers. He said: And the fact that Eléonora's ring finger is growing so naturally on her hand is because next week Jean-Baptiste is going to put a golden ring on it.

He paused and while the rest of us drank wine from Lisbon the mine owner took a sip of his potion in order to subdue his nerves. He wanted to express his disagreement but before he had a chance to speak the philosopher continued. He explained that back when he had been affiliated with the Dutch royal house he had gone for a walk one evening along the beach when a large number of courtiers caught up with him. They wanted to know whether he had seen the King's dog that had run away. He asked whether it was a dachshund with a bad leg that had recently had puppies. They immediately wanted to know where he had seen it and to their astonishment he said that he had never seen it.

Whereupon my fiance put down her hand of cards on the table. I remember that on that day she was wearing an unusual amount of rouge on her cheeks. I myself had read and heard the story, and many others that were similar, beforehand.

It is simple logic for children and old ladies, he explained. The royal house had always kept dachshunds, long sausage-like creatures and which had been reconfirmed to him by the animal tracks he had seen in the sand because there was a certain amount of length between its front and hind legs. But that wasn't all. Some light and narrow grooves in some of the small sand hills indicated that it was a female dog whose breasts were hanging because it had just had puppies a few days earlier.

At the same time I noticed, he said, that the sand was less furrowed under one paw than it was under the other three, making me realize that the dog of the exalted King was—pardon me—limping.

My fiance and her mother clapped their hands spontaneously. But their enthusiasm immediately disappeared when we caught sight of a large, pitch dark figure standing on the town square just outside the window. And I never did get the chance to put a wedding ring on Eléonora's finger.

THE BLACK MAN, whom I recognized as being the shaft overseer who had lowered us down into the mine was invited inside. I still recall how we sat assembled around the card table as he stood there in the middle of the room trying to find the right words to convey what had transpired.

He told us how earlier that day he had been walking along the town square when a passing woman let her handkerchief drop before him. He explained how he picked it up and followed her. Every time he lagged a little too far behind she would stop up as though waiting for him to catch up with her. At one point he wanted to call to her whereupon she placed her very erect index finger on her lips, letting him know that he was to keep quiet. At the periphery of the city, in the slums, she had disappeared into a lone house in which a man had been sitting at one of the windows smoking. Down a secret, dark stairway he ended up in a basement which was cold and humid. She was nowhere to be seen.

In the basement there were open tubs filled with apples and sealed barrels filled with sour, foaming cider. It was dark but somewhere in the distance a flickering light could just be discerned.

I find it appropriate to, once again, stress the fact that I didn't like the shaft overseer. I knew that Bertel Gessler, which was his name, had, in his earlier days, been a well-proportioned and handsome man who had enjoyed a position of considerable responsibility as overseer of the mine owner's house. I had been informed that about two years ago Gessler started frequenting my father-in-law-to-be's private home quite a bit. According to the young man's own account it had to do with the fact that his hunting dog had taken a liking to the pet dog that the mine owner had bought for his wife. But one day when the mine owner had come home he discovered that there were other things that had been taken a liking to as well. What it was exactly that had transpired I'm not certain but on several occasions the mine owner assured me that her reproductive organs were untouched and he would make sure that they continued to be so. In his rage he had killed Gessler's dog that had been running around freely and unaware in a small yard outside and Bertel Gessler was subsequently stationed in the dirty mine hole.

He stood there in the living room now like a dark and ugly shadow of himself as a small pool accumulated under him on the newly washed floors. And he smelled. Let's put it this way: the stale earthy smell in the basement I myself would soon be inhaling clung to him.

He explained that he had gone in the direction of the light, which was a very natural thing to do, and had discovered an opening: a tunnel with small torches on either side. He understood that this was the mine's passage system that had slowly hollowed out the soil under the ground below the city and which he was now entering. He recognized dormitories and hearths where the miners could warm up and make food. There were no people anywhere in sight and the usual sounds of chopping and shovels were nowhere to be heard either. When he walked long enough he reached the place where the crack in the well had occurred. That was where he caught sight of Ansaldo, the little man with the blood-seeped bandages. He stood with his back to him as he was busy bricking up the hole.

Gessler had approached him, called to him, spoken to him but Ansaldo had made no reply. When he got up close to him he had placed his hand on his shoulder. This light touch had resulted in a response he hadn't thought possible. Ansaldo fell immediately to the ground as had he been swept off his feet. Then his body began convulsing wildly from great spasms and yellow foam developed around his mouth. He hadn't dared touch him and when the bodily fluids began seeping through the many bandages that Ansaldo always bore, Gessler had run away.

II:C

THE HOUSE WAS EMPTY and locked up, the only thing we were able to find was an empty tobacco pouch on the sidewalk. The robust main door was blocked by thin boards and the house shutters were closed. It was as though no one had ever lived in the house. It was wedged between two buildings that were much taller.

I noticed that melting snow was dripping from the roof and I pointed it out. The mine owner believed that that was an indication that there was a source of heat in there and that there was no doubt that there was a secret in the house that was being concealed from the rest of the world. The philosopher first suggested that the melting snow had been caused by the change in weather since it had grown considerably less cold. But when the mine owner then pointed out that the colorless facade emitted a higher temperature the philosopher, in turn, pointed out the fact that there was a bakery right next door and that it most probably used this closed building for its big ovens that had to be situated in there somewhere.

While they were busy championing each their own opinion the black man had started working on the door with his sword. He placed the hard and wide steel blade between the door casing and the nailed boards and broke them off one by one. When he was done he took an ax and went at the door until it broke. Then he let out a roar as he placed his hands on both sides of the broken door and jumped inside. At first I thought it was an attempt to frighten away any possible enemies that might be waiting inside but it turned out that he had torn one of his hands on a board. It may seem tedious including such details but they are important for properly understanding how things developed later on and I can also say with some certainty that we didn't see a single pea pod or seed pod in the house though I am certain that there must have been some.

First we searched the ground floor. There wasn't much furniture in the house and I was under the impression that all that was left were fixtures that the former inhabitants hadn't wanted to take with them. The tapestry was old and semi-rotten.

We entered a bigger room in which a woman was sitting on a chair. She was wearing a cotton shirt which was pale-yellow as had she been perspiring in it for several days. Underneath it I was able to discern the silhouette of her poitrine. She observed our presence disinterestedly.

I asked Gessler whether that was the woman he had followed but he was so preoccupied with inspecting his damaged hand that he didn't hear me.

Then she rose and walked over to the darkest part of the room. Her body was emaciated and at the same time heavy. I was filled with great unease when I saw that the bundle she took down that had been hanging from a nail in the wall was a baby wrapped in cloth. She sat back down in the chair and placed the baby under her shirt to her breast. It began sucking in her nourishment with great appetite.

I realized that what Gessler had stumbled upon was a whorehouse which the underground miners could go to when they needed to escape the hard grind of their work and I realized that the babies here were hung up on the wall so as not to be in the way when the women served their customers.

The philosopher explained to me that it was common practice among nomads to transport infants in small packages made of material and that it also ensured that their limbs grew straight. He also said that in those areas where swaddling was common it was teeming with hunchbacks, cripples and men with withered members.

And then the strangest thing occurred: he pulled out his sharp sword and stuck it in Gessler's stomach, all the way to the shaft, whereupon Gessler dropped dead on the spot.

AS SOON AS THE PHILOSOPHER HAD TOLD the reason why the shaft overseer had to die we spent two hours blocking the descent to the cellar with rubble. Then we gathered as much flammable material as we could find and put it in piles around the house. Then we set it on fire and went outside. The woman nursing her child and Gessler's dead corpse were still inside there. Without needing to exchange any words all three of us knew that we had done the right thing. The blood that had seeped from Gessler's hand when he injured it hadn't been red, like it is in normal humans, but resembled a whitish milk-like substance.

As we stood there watching the house go in flames the mine owner said to us that, despite everything, he hoped that Gessler's soul was now on its way up to Our Lord. The philosopher said that he simply could not subscribe to the idea that a soul, who was, after all, merely visiting here on earth, would voluntarily choose to inhabit a human frame full of excrement, urine and stinking entrails, and so he simply didn't believe in them.

When the house had burnt down to the ground we all three got into the sleigh beneath a thick layer of bear hide whereupon we headed toward the mine opening. We knew that we were forced, once and for all, to shut down the source from which all the madness seemed to derive.

The first thing we did when we got there was to cut the cable to the basket, which was a very sensible thing to do. It was now impossible to come up or go down and while the philosopher, who was good with chemicals, started casting a funnel of lead we were able to hear the workers starting to gather below us. Shouts of curses and damnations could be heard. But we continued working steadfastly and calmly and when we were done with the lid we put it in place by joint effort.

We decided to go to the pub. We needed a quick one. As we were being served steeped stock fish and warm oat cakes the mine owner complained about the problems he now was facing. He was employed in the King's service and he said that that which we had done would cost him dearly. He knew that not only did the Swedish king have great debt items in Lübeck but he also needed all the income he could get to build up an army.

He was deeply affected by what had happened. Which was understandable, all three of us were, but nevertheless, he irritated me. We had much graver things to think about than his personal concerns. And to what degree would become apparent to me just a few moments later.

When I grew tired of listening to his elegy I went over to the window and looked across the Swedish plain. We were to ride yet another hour in order to get back to the estate in time. I noticed that the horse that had pulled us through the snow stood with its hind leg and tail lifted. Dung came pouring out. There was already a pile of steaming horse droppings in the snow behind it. It was clearly frightened of something which I didn't know what was, but as is commonly known, animals are often better able to sense things than we humans.

The mine owner continued talking behind me. I remember he said that he too was nervous that the local peasants were going to turn on him since all the great losses would force the king to collect higher taxes.

Then, far in the horizon, I caught sight of the first torches in the thick evening fog and soon I also saw the appearance of the first of many pallid black figures. They came on horseback and on foot and more and more of them continued to come. To be honest, I don't know how many there were, but no less than one hundred is my guess. To this very day I have managed to convince myself that they were singing a song of mourning that grew louder and louder the closer they got, which they did very rapidly.

II:D

III
THE COFFIN

III:A

THE GATES TO THE OUTSIDE WORLD were simply shut. We weren't entirely sure what it was we had seen but we knew that we would do everything in our power to avoid getting into contact with it. At that point we assumed that the miners must have managed to crawl their way up out of the hole and that they were now coming to take their revenge.

My wedding was called off. It didn't make the slightest bit of difference to me. I never did get the obligatory tingling sensation in my testicles when I was in the company of Eléonora. Meanwhile most of the guests had arrived so we were now a huge number of people behind the walls. Not that there wasn't enough food because there was, even though it mostly consisted of potatoes and apples.

The philosopher and I would do our daily rounds in the inner courtyard where we, as we heard the ice cracking and crinkling on the biggest of the lakes because the weather was growing warmer, discussed the situation in which we currently found ourselves. And we weren't the only ones. People were talking. It was said that the souls of the mine workers had grown wet and they had been sent down by God in order to punish human greed and our inordinate love of luxury. That obviously also included the mine owner and I heard rumors that if we just opened the gates and threw him out to his fate then everything would be all right again. I didn't tell him that those kinds of ideas were circulating. He was already beside himself. I knew that he was inspecting his chamber pot every morning to see what his inner organs had managed to eliminate in the course of the night and that he had suddenly prohibited his daughter, my coming bride, from playing with her Marionettes. He was changing his ways and he wasn't the only one. A fire would be lit on a specially set up bonfire several times a day in order to cleanse the air and people would eat blueberries and consume sour vinegar because it was said that doing so would keep the soul dry.

When we had been isolated from the rest of the world for a good week or so crows, ravens and some other big and strange looking foreign birds settled on the walls in large numbers. They sat there looking down at us as though they were merely waiting for us to collapse from fever and other symptoms so they could start feeding on us.

The philosopher tried to talk some sense into people. He pointed out that the same thing happened every year, namely, that the warm weather brought the birds from the south to the north and that they would go in the opposite direction come autumn. Nothing could be more natural, he said, adding, not until the day dogs start laying eggs will I be alarmed.

He maintained that he still hadn't seen or heard anything that fell outside the bounds of what could be naturally explained with reason. After having said that a considerable amount of times it was suggested that as a result he, brave soul that he was, would be the right one to venture beyond the gates and examine the lay of the land. After several days of heated debating he consented. And I went with him.

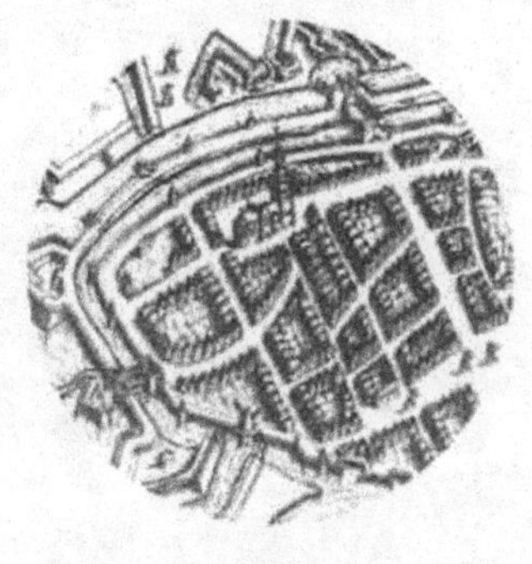

III:B

WE DIDN'T SEE ANY PEOPLE when we arrived at the town. We rode directly toward the square. We dismounted our horses and gazed across the open and deserted area where fruit, fish and various forms of tools were normally sold. We didn't speak to one another. The philosopher was agitated and angry and I can't say that I didn't understand him. Just prior to when we left the mine owner's estate we received a message that one of the servants had discovered large, gray eggs in the hay which the dogs had slept in. Even thought the situation was grave and the sense of fear pervaded everyone, they apparently couldn't help teasing my traveling companion. I know that there had also been much talk of his black, pointed hat, something which I should have drawn his attention to.

The philosopher asked me whether I had noticed that all the doors to the houses facing the market square were open. I hadn't. The shutters hadn't been closed either.

We began examining the houses, one at a time, and they were just as empty as the streets and alleys. Everything had been left untouched, as though all the inhabitants had simply got up and left whatever it was they had been busy doing at the time. In a few of the places the hearth was still warm when you placed your hand on it.

Not until we came to the most impressive looking of the houses did we find something of interest. It belonged to a rich merchant's family that originally came from Bulgaria. The floors in the dining rooms were shiny and there were not only painted tapestries but embroidered ones as well that were so thick that they could keep out the cold.

The philosopher told me that the merchant's daughter was a desirable catch. She was not only renowned for her beauty but also for her great intelligence as well as the fact that she had the ability to sympathize with and respect other people's weaknesses. The philosopher also said that rumor had it that her father held exquisite evening balls with music and dancing in her honor. He did so in the hopes of finding someone who would be worthy of his daughter and who was able to pass every kind of test. But he never approved of anyone. He let her walk on the Persian carpets and rose leaves, untouched.

Already on the way down to the cellar I heard this strange crackling noise that I will never forget until my dying day. It reminded me of those grasshoppers in the south that rub their legs against one another beneath the summer sun, which in turn made me think of all the tiny jaws in a swarm of bees biting into old wood except the sound came from another kind of insect. From the walls and ceiling there hung armadillos like the one the mine owner had pointed out in the forest. Most of them, which were the size of a dessert plate, were slowly crawling around amongst one another making it hard to tell them apart.

The philosopher believed that they were busy digging. He who knew so much about zoology explained to me that they used their front limbs to break the soil and their hind legs to kick the same soil behind them. I didn't share his enthusiasm in the least bit. They were grayish-black and their soft tissues were protected by a back shield and horny layer that made me think of the mine workers. He also said that their offspring were born in special combs in the earth and at the time of birth they were only covered with a soft, leathery skin that didn't grow hard until they were full-grown.

I honestly don't know why he said all of this. The only way I can explain it now, in retrospect, is that he didn't want to see that which he actually was seeing and it is for that reason that it is me and not him who is writing all of this because the time has come for the whole thing to be brought to light. Instead, the philosopher has said he will compose an article for the encyclopedia that is being compiled in our homeland about the little island out in the bay. All I can do is wish him the best of luck with it and apart from that continue with my own efforts.

I didn't for one moment think that the armadillos or the Lapis Larvae were busy digging. My thought was that they in unison were busy consuming something underneath them and I was convinced that that which they were eating weren't stones but the merchant's beautiful daughter who, for some reason or other, hadn't managed to escape like the others.

WHEN WE RETURNED to the estate we were greeted by the mine owner and his wife and daughter. Our hostess wore a tall wig and and heavy makeup as though she were going to a ball. At first I thought that they wanted to know what we had seen and heard. But they didn't. Instead they wanted to deliver an unwelcome piece of news which we could have done without.

The mine owner asked us to follow him, which we did, and as we walked I had the opportunity to tell about what we had seen at Falun. Both ladies lifted their dresses when I described how one of the armadillos that had been lying on the basement stairs had suddenly pulled its armored leg back and tucked it under itself so that it was fully shielded all the way around.

The mine owner showed us into one of his most recent buildings, a chapel which had been built in keeping with the fashion of the day which included many vivid colors and colorful paintings on the walls. Sure enough, just as he had said, the marble coffin was open and that which it had contained was gone.

I looked down into the empty sarcophagus and didn't know what to believe. All I can say is that I became greatly alarmed.

Then the philosopher began to speak and asked us to relax. He said that when events happen independent of one another in time and space it may well be difficult to find a sensible cause and effect but that is not the same as had there not been any at all. When it is raining toads on the field it is not a warning about an upcoming misfortune but because the windy weather has blown and carried the amphibians from a nearby lake only to drop them in some other spot. And that's that.

It is sensus communis, natural common sense, he said, thereby concluding his argument.

As to which the mine owner said that he couldn't at all see how the situation we were in now had anything to do with frogs falling from the sky. Or apples for that matter.

I can't say anything other than that I was inclined to agree with him.

I remember that we had gone outside when this exchange of views took place and I was worried that the discussion was going to develop into an outright brawl. The weather was very warm and it became obvious that the two gentlemen were hot-headed.

I know that the philosopher had also said something else that would prove to have a direct impact on the subsequent course of events but I no longer recall what it was. Perhaps I will have the opportunity to ask him later tonight when he returns. He is still running around among the beef cattle on the living island that has emerged in the bay because seeds and kernels have landed on the surface of the water and have mixed with shifting sands. The island moves whenever the wind blows through the tree tops.

The man from Rouen simply can't seem to get enough. He is determined to get the most that he possibly can out of everything. For the last couple of hours I have been able to discern the glow of his swinging lantern up from my tower room.

IV
THE BET

IV:A

SO THE SARCOPHAGUS was open and empty and the following day the weather was horrible. The rain was pouring down so we remained indoors and passed the hours discussing what we could expect from whatever it was that had been locked inside the coffin. Without going into too many details I think it is safe to say that the mine owner was under the impression that we had every reason to fear the evil one's helper who was now running about freely somewhere in our proximity. It was with great emotion that he told us, which is to say the philosopher, myself and five others who had gathered in the dining room, that the offspring that results from when an angel frequents human company is capable of piercing and consuming its way inside an otherwise perfectly natural and healthy human body.

However, the philosopher, who right away saw that there was absolutely no reason to incite people any further, everyone was scared enough of each other as it was, refused to hear a word of it. I no longer recall what was said. The rain was pouring down in buckets outside the windows. At some point the mine owner, who stuck to his guns, brought in some "household" beer. As his servants poured the beer from the pitchers e, lamenting over the fact that the beer had a funny aftertaste because the townspeople had started doing their laundry at the very spot where the water was fetched from the brewery, the mine owner presented the hypothesis that the nursing woman whom we had seen in the basement in the house in town was most probably an angel who had mated with the devilish black sinner who had worked in the mine. He was certain, he said, that the nursing milk that she provided to the children had had the same yellowish color as the fluid that had seeped through Ansaldo's bandages, the blood that had dripped from Gessler's wound and the droppings that had fallen from the shitting bird that had flown about in the room.

We had now reached a turning point. Again, I don't remember all the details, but the mine owner's crazy yet at the same time somehow inescapable assumption threw, I could see, the philosopher slightly off. I would be lying if I said that his words didn't evoke a strange and very unpleasant response within me.

The philosopher managed to summon the necessary strength to remain calm. He got up and said that this would have to be put to a test. The time has now come, he said, to evaluate the situation and once and for all to dismiss these dark and dangerous thoughts. Whereupon he compared the mine owner's observations with a tuberous plant he had once seen in an old water hole which had both been sprouting and rotting at the same time.

It was now the mine owner's turn to get up. The beer was beginning to affect him. He stood on his legs shakily. Yes, he proclaimed, I will gladly pick up the gauntlet.

The next thing that happened was that the two angry men sat down in the room next door to figure how to settle the dispute between them. The rest of us continued drinking beer and looking out at the rain.

Two hours later they returned. We looked at them in great anticipation. The result of their efforts became the following agreement: Using Pliny the Elder's *Naturalis historia,* one of the works which the philosopher had brought with him, as their point of departure, then all living creatures within the walls were to be examined and if there wasn't anything inside of them that there shouldn't be then the mine owner would humbly acknowledge his defeat. He would also, without hesitation, hand over the earnings the mine had yielded the previous year to the philosopher and his faithful companion, in other words, me. Should they, on the other hand, manage to find traces of the anemic fluid and could prove that it derived from the devil himself then the philosopher, who, it would seem, had had a few too many beers at that point, agreed to be beheaded.

WHAT I WOULD CALL a sense of anticipatory entrepreneurship was beginning to develop among the five men who were privy to the bet. As soon as the rain stopped they got busy erecting a small scaffold. The mine owner hung a bullseye made of hay up on one of the first beams that was raised and continued his old passion of shooting with bows and arrows. Eléonora and her mother, who were pacing back and forth, arm in arm, would stop every now and then and recite paternosters and avemarias whenever they passed the building activity.

The philosopher and I had no time for pranks. The man from Rouen had taken it upon himself to lead the examination and he had selected me as his helper. Which I had no problem with. He was very motivated for the task for, as he himself put it, not only was this the big test for him on a personal level but also for the laws which reality is subject to. Today, in retrospect, I am convinced that he saw the upcoming work as a way to force the world back on track, upon which, according to him, it had its natural order.

We borrowed a small bow scimitar from the surgeon and the first thing we did was to examine some horses prancing around in their fenced in area and behaving as though they were reindeer. Still, there was nothing strange about them nor the other mute animals which we either killed or cut through with a knife and left alive.

Then the philosopher asked me to complete a list of all the people around the estate. He wanted to know where they lived, what sort of occupation they had, their ages and other things. I asked him what he needed to know those things for. He explained to me that each individual person has received from nature, already prior to his birth, a certain destiny. One will become an equerry, another a soldier, a third a banker and so on. That is why, he explained, they all at some point or other begin to manifest that which they have been selected to do and that is why we must try to keep an eye on the individual who hasn't quite managed to fulfill his ordained role but is constantly straightening his sweater as if it wasn't sitting properly.

And so we did. We sought out the individuals who were odd and deviated from the norm in some way or other, but all of them we could cross off my list. Neither was there anyone on the estate who was able to produce a single drop of the fluidy paleness we were searching for when we cut them in the finger.

The philosopher tried not to show any feelings but it became increasingly clear that he, as the hours passed, grew more and more cheerful the closer we got to the ultimate triumph and to the great prize that lay within reach. Finally, there was only the miller left.

IV:B

Koege Bay, Kirchenborg Castle, Denmark,
  June 3, 1749, night/morning, 14°

THE MILLER WAS STANDING in the doorway when we arrived. His little house was located so close to the windmill that its broad arms almost hit the roof on their descent down.

I have been waiting for you, he said and ushered us in. We entered a room in which the ceiling was so low that the philosopher was unable to stand upright but was forced to duck his head. A woman lay in a bed box with only her head showing above a tightly tucked-in bed sheet that was spread so flatly on the bed that it was hard to imagine that there was an actual body underneath it. She had long blond hair and very large eyes. Behind her, toward the wall, lay a boy with black hair. I imagine he was around three-four years old. I remember thinking that the woman bore a certain resemblance to the prostitute we had seen in the house in town. I said so to the philosopher. To which he made no response. It didn't seem to interest him.

Now the miller began to speak: my first wife died in childbirth when my son was born many years ago and even though my son was very close in following his mother to the grave we were, nonetheless, allowed to keep him. But these days it takes both a husband and wife to run a household like this, so I remarried.

He touched her hair with the tips of his fingers and I could not only sense but also hear the big arms of the mill as they moved past us, one by one, just on the other side of the very thin roof. The single window in the room was partially covered by corn bags that had been sewn together.

Despite the fact that I have ploughed in her all the energy that I could muster, he continued, it has not resulted in any more offspring and her mouth is so small that you can barely even get a finger in there.

He then ordered her out of the bed and she slowly crawled out and stood up, scrawny and staggering, in the middle of the floor wearing nothing but her unbuttoned underwear and a white tunic with sleeves which in my homeland is called a *Chemise de nuit*. It wasn't necessary to make incisions in her, I noticed, because she was in the middle of her lunar cycle and the blood that ran out of her was red and brown, which was the proper color.

We then turned our attention to the boy, but the miller waved us away.

In a disagreeable torrent of words he apologized for the situation life had put him in, he compared himself with Josef whose seven fat cows were consumed by the seven ugly and skinny cows that ascended from the rush of the Nile and it became gradually clear to us that when it came to his son, who was of his own flesh and blood, we would have to pay for being allowed to examine him.

The miller and his family were the last ones left on our list and I assume that that was what prompted the philosopher to reach for his leather wallet. The miller immediately shook his round, coarse head as soon as he realized that what he was being offered were French sous. The philosopher immediately began making estimates and calculations to demonstrate all the beautiful things that could be acquired for those sous in France but, as the miller responded, there was nothing that indicated that he was going to France in the near future.

The one who squeezes the bread crust so hard that the insides crumble is squeezing it too hard, said the philosopher as he, I noticed, tightened his grip on the scimitar and the boy crawled further into the bed box almost as though he was trying to hide.

I REMEMBER THAT ON THAT NIGHT we were seated in the big banquet hall, and I remember that we were served pâtes, ham and cheese. We sat alternating between talking and eating in silence, as one typically does in those types of situations.

Naturally I noticed that the mine owner wasn't in a particularly good mood, which I initially ascribed to the defeat that had befallen him. Apart from that, I couldn't deny the fact it gave me a little pleasure to witness.

I recall seeing him dab himself behind the ears several times during the evening with the warm wine in the pot. He had run out of the elixir and due to our situation it was impossible for him to restock it. Meanwhile it was to become apparent that the mine owner's restlessness derived from something entirely different. I grasped it immediately upon seeing his wife, Eléonora's mother, step into the banquet hall. She was powdered and her hair was done up and she placed the small jar she was always carrying with her on the floor, whereupon she started circulating amongst the guests while smoothing out her dress. When she, which was naturally considered to be rather awkward, curtseyed to her husband he said: You have managed to capture and keep my heart in your prison, filling me with a constant urge while you prowl around like a bitch in heat.

Since that remark, due to his way of delivering it, struck me as being more than a mere whim on his part, I left my seat next to the philosopher in order to better hear the exchange that was now taking place.

She: Is it possible to have a reasonable conversation with you?

He. I am always receptive to reason.

She: I am a loving wife and not a tramp.

He: Then tell me now where you have been keeping house.

She: Ask those rats that suggested hanging a bell from the cat's tail, was her response.

Whereupon the jar tipped over as if on its own accord or perhaps she was the one who did it as a means to escape the interrogation she was being subjected to, in any event, the liquid with the healing properties poured out, spreading out like a thick pool of water on the floor.

A FEW MOMENTS LATER we were standing in the antechamber of the field hospital without having entered it. I had not included the soldier in on our list since he did not belong to the group residing at the estate. That was, of course, a mistake, I realize that now. The philosopher did not reproach me for it then nor has he done so since.

I could clearly tell that he was nervous for what was awaiting us and all I can say is that I understood him. But that which we were about to witness would overshadow our wildest imaginations and the whole way in which things were about to unfold is essentially what has compelled me to write all of this down.

I remember that there was a sweet smell at the field camp, like the powder used against fungus and infectious germs. It had not only been sprinkled on the floor but smeared on the walls as well. We looked around.

Bonjour, a dry voice said from inside one of the wards.

We looked inside. That was where he was sitting. The soldier. In the bed, dressed in rags, with a black hood covering his head and a spice pouch hanging from his neck.

Of how can I be of service? he asked.

I remained standing in the doorway, but the philosopher entered the room and sat down on a stool next to the sick bed. He placed the scimitar on the floor.

To be perfectly honest, I had difficulty concentrating on the questions that the man from Rouen posed and the responses that the soldier gave him because as they were speaking something or other told me that I had met him before. I couldn't see his face. It was hidden under the hood. I now stepped into the room whereupon the unpleasant odor which he exuded entered my nose. He truly stank as had he been lying in a coffin below the ground for one hundred years.

Then the philosopher wanted to know how he had become injured and the response he gave was that he had been shot in the knee on the battlefield where later he had woken up beneath a heap of corpses and wounded soldiers on the bed of a wagon.

Naturally I realized that he was full of it. For one thing, there were no battles in the part of Europe we were in, neither in Lifland nor Kurland, and for another, I was suddenly no longer in doubt as to his identity. In the course of two quick paces I was standing by his bed and in a single movement tore off the hood from his head.

I jumped back in utter horror. Despite the fact that half his head was covered with boils and raging smallpox and that most of the tip of his nose had been consumed by the plague, I could easily tell that it was, in fact, the spice merchant's son who was sitting in the bed before me.

He broke down in tears, covered his ruined face with his hands and told his story, which I shall now record from memory.

Shortly after we arrived in Calais, he began, I started noticing the first signs, but I didn't want to see them even though they clearly were there and once I was sitting in the sailor's boat on my way to the embarkation, well, I saw no reason to return to land where you were waiting for me. It was too late for my part.

The illness had seriously broken out after we had been out at sea for a week. I was quarantined, but at that point I had already managed to contaminate most of the remaining crew and it wasn't long before they were all lying down and writhing like worms up on deck.

He had disembarked in Caracas, he said, where he had visited a surgeon and found an extract dispensed by a pharmacy. This had helped him to recover so much that he was able to begin his long journey home, which was more than tantamount to Odysseus' journey home to Penelope and his home of Ithaca. He had witnessed a farm burning down on the Spanish part of the island of St. Domingo where a negro by the name of Houango had murdered 40 white people with his machete. He had also bought soap in Marseilles, seen a beached whale and had, once he finally reached Italy, joined company with two humble gentlemen of honor who turned out to be highway robbers. In retrospect, he realized that they had already from their first encounter planned to kill him and rob him of his possessions. The more devious of the two had even had the audacity to say to the spice merchant's son, who, during his morning prayers, was always asking God to help him find a proper resting place for the coming night, that he, who knew perfectly well how the spice merchant's son's days would end, was certain that he was going to get an even better night's rest than he himself even if he chose not to pray. As is evident from my rendering, his account wasn't particularly coherent, but from what I could infer the two thieves had taken out their wooden clubs when they, that same evening, had reached a deserted ford. Our countryman did not die from the many blows he received but instead had fortune on his side. He had awoken naked and, to his great, surprise, in a beautiful villa. An older marchioness had discovered him lying lifeless on the ground and her servants had carried him and brought him to a bed, whereupon she got busy preparing a lavish supper for him and afterward took him with her to the town square where ten soldiers could be seen dragging the two robbers. It turned out that they had not only been forced to spend the night in a filthy cell, but were also now being led to the scaffold to be executed by hanging.

Now it just so happened that the mine owner showed up at the doorway with raging eyes, his nostrils palpitating and his bow drawn back. I don't recall all the details. Everything was going so fast at this point. We shouted. I have, of course, numerous times since considered what I could have done. I was the one standing closest to the mine owner. Lord knows that, no matter what, the spice merchant's son was the first in line to die. Death will eventually overtake us all at some time or other but, thanks to the mine owner's stubbornness and jealousy the arrow sped through the air with great force and we never did get a chance to receive the answers to all of our questions.

The spice merchant's son was hit in the chest. The arrow had pierced through him so deeply that not even the feathers were visible. At first I heard a hissing sound and then I saw the blood seeping through his rags. It wasn't red but had the same yellow color as the liquid that had seeped through Ansaldo's bandages, the blood from Gessler's incision and the droppings that had fallen from the bird.

ONCE YOU HAVE raised your hand to strike a blow it hurts if you end up missing and hitting the empty air, the mine owner said without meaning anything in particular by those words. He had resigned himself to the agreement that had been made. He had taken a life he had had no right to take and so he now had to abandon taking the life he could have taken, namely the philosopher's.

The spice merchant's son's dead body, save for the head, was destroyed by being thrown into an abandoned old well which was later thoroughly sealed off, which is to say according to the same principles we had used when we had closed off the hole to the mine.

Prior to that the mine owner's wife had decapitated the spice merchant's son and cleansed the head with her tears and later placed it in the jar she had used to bring him ointment. She filled it with soil and took a basil seed from Salerno that had been in the spice bag that had hung from his neck and added it to the soil. She added more tears as well as rose water. Already the following day a lush plant had sprung up from the soil and even though it had a bit of the after-smell that reminded me of the illness that had spread in our hometown which we will now soon be revisiting, it had its own special tinge which I shall never forget.

Yes, we are returning home. Earlier today there arrived the much anticipated letter from France. My brother has informed me that the quarantine is now over and I no longer see any reason to delay the journey now that my story has been told in its entirety. I can hear the philosopher in the room next door. He is busy bundling his odds and ends and he is humming in the same way that he did when we were walking about the estate, cutting into people and animals with the surgeon's saber.

Fig. 1.

O:B

NINA SOKOL is a poet and translator in the midst of translating novels, short stories. plays and poems by Danish writers. She was a grant poet-in-residence at The Vermont Studio Center in 2011. She has received several grants from the Danish Art's Council to translate plays, including a play written by the fairy tale writer H.C. Andersen which was published by the journal "InTranslation." She has also translated an excerpt from one of the winning novels of last year›s EU Prize for Literature (Danish, 2016) as well as translated such authors Niviaq Korneliussen and Bjørn Rasmussen. Her own poems have appeared in American journals, including Miller's Pond and the Hiram Poetry Review and a collection was published by Lapwing Publications in Belfast, Ireland (2015).

ROBERT ZOLA CHRISTENSEN Ph.D., has written more than 30 books in both non-fiction and fiction (novels, crime fiction, children books). His works have been translated into several languages, including German, French, Serbian, Russian and Swedish. His latest novel, *No Balloons* (2017), explores the different lifestyles in Scandinavia, political correctness and the role of man today. Originally from Denmark, Robert Zola Christensen is currently an Associate Professor at Lund University in Sweden.

0:C